Thing in the Fridge

by Susan Knight
illustrated by Luke Jurevicius
and Jason Pamment

Characters

Thing

Blob

Contents

Chapter 1

Born in a Mess

It all began when someone turned off the power by mistake. In the freezer the ice cream melted. The ground meat dribbled. The frozen peas fell apart and went mushy.

The ice cream oozed into the ground meat. The ground meat dribbled into the peas. The peas drank it up.

Everything got mixed up in a slimy lake. It became warm and sticky and smelly. Strange blobs began to grow.

In one of those blobs, Thing was born. She was white like the ice cream. She was covered in gray fuzz. She had eyes like peas. And she hopped.

Suddenly, the freezer door opened. The light flashed in Thing's pea-green eyes. She hid in a corner.

"Pew! What a stink! Who turned off the power?" yelled an angry voice. "The food is all spoiled."

A huge hand jerked in and out of the freezer. It scraped out the mess. A big wet cloth wiped the walls. Thing stayed hiding in her corner. Slam! The door was shut.

All was quiet. Thing came out of her hiding place. She looked around. Her world was bare and empty, and now it was getting cold.

Suddenly, the door opened again. Thing ran for cover.

Food was thrown into the freezer—packs of peas, a whole fish, a tub of ice cream. Slam! The door was shut again.

Thing kicked the pack of peas. She licked a bit of ice cream stuck on the lid. It was getting colder. Soon everything was white and frosty. Thing curled up and went to sleep, but not for long.

The door opened again. Then it closed. Then it opened again! Thing got tired of hiding. She couldn't sleep in peace.

She skated on ice cubes. She slid down fish scales. She bounced on steak until it was frozen. Once she even swam in some fresh soup. But in the end, everything froze and became white and hard.

Thing was bored.

Chapter 2

A Buzzy Visitor

"Hey!" said a buzzy voice in the dark. "Hey! Let me out! It's really cold in here!"

A fly was trapped in the freezer.

"Help! This is a mistake. I wanted the fridge, not the freezer."

The fly moved more and more slowly. He fell over. He kicked his legs in the air.

"There's nothing good in here," he croaked. "All the best stuff is down below —sausages, cake, eggs, vegetables, cheese." He blinked and froze solid.

Thing had been listening. "Down below" sounded like a great place!

"I must go there," she said. "I want to know about vegetables and sausages. I want to know about cake and eggs. I want to know about cheese!"

Chapter 3

Down Below

Thing hopped to the freezer door and waited. Soon enough the door opened, and Thing slipped over the edge. She slid down an icicle onto a flat place.

It was the meat tray, full of soft, pink sausages. Thing had never seen sausages before.

"Hooray!" she said. "This must be cake!"

She ate some. It was sticky and raw.

"I don't think much of cake," she said.
"What else is here?"

Thing looked over the edge of the tray. Everything was full of color and funny shapes. She saw a bowl of eggs.

"Hooray!" she said. "They must be vegetables!"

She slid down a sausage toward the bowl. Oops! Too slippery! Thing fell into the bowl of eggs. Crack! Crack! Crack!

Thing began to thrash about. She gulped and blew bubbles and yelled. As she whipped her arms, the egg whites got thicker and thicker. At last they were so thick and fluffy, she could stand on them.

Thing spit out the taste of egg.

"Pah! Blah!" she said. "I don't think much of vegetables."

Thing hopped along a street of tall milk cartons. She came to a plate of lemons.

"Hooray! These must be eggs," she said.

She poked a lemon with her spiky finger. Juice came out, and Thing licked her finger.

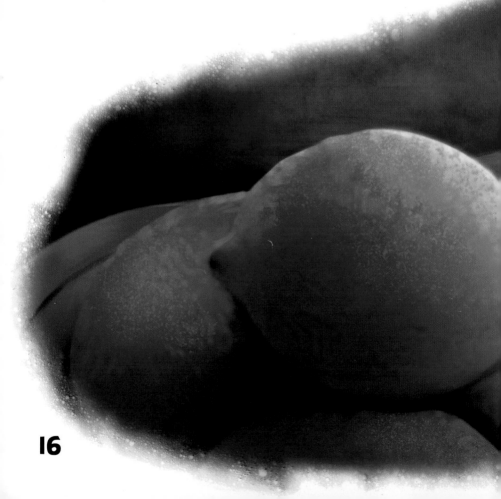

"SSSSSsspppitttt!" said Thing, making a
sour face. "I don't think much of eggs."

"Now I want to find the cheese."

Chapter 4

Thing Finds the Blob

"Cheese?" growled a thick voice. "Did someone say *cheeeeeeeese?*"

A fat yellow shape slid off a shelf. It had a big mouth with sharp teeth. It had dark spots, and it stank.

"What do *you* know about cheese?" roared the Blob. It snapped its teeth at Thing.

Thing hid behind a broken eggshell.

"Not much," she said. "Does it taste good?"

"Do you want cheese with *bite*?" the Blob said, getting angrier. "Pizza cheese? *Smelly* cheese?"

"Yes, please," said Thing. "I'd like a piece of cheese!"

"You *really* want cheese?" shouted the Blob. "I'll give you cheese!"

The Blob rushed at Thing and knocked her over.

Thing grabbed a carrot and swung it at the Blob. "Get back, get back, you . . . you . . . Blob!"

Blob chased Thing all around the fridge. They ran along the shelf. They ran past the butter and milk cartons. They ran down into the vegetable crisper. Through celery and spuds, the Blob chased Thing with growls and snaps.

But brave Thing would not stop, and they ran all the way back to the top shelf again.

Suddenly small cheers came from around them. Insects had crawled out of the vegetables to watch the chase. They sat on the shelf and shouted.

"Get the Blob!"

"He's a stinker!"

"Go, Thing, go!"

This made the Blob furious. It roared and leaped at Thing. Thing swung her carrot, but it broke. The Blob grabbed her.

"Help!" Thing shouted.

The bugs and beetles rushed to help. But just then the door opened, and the Blob and Thing fell out of the fridge.

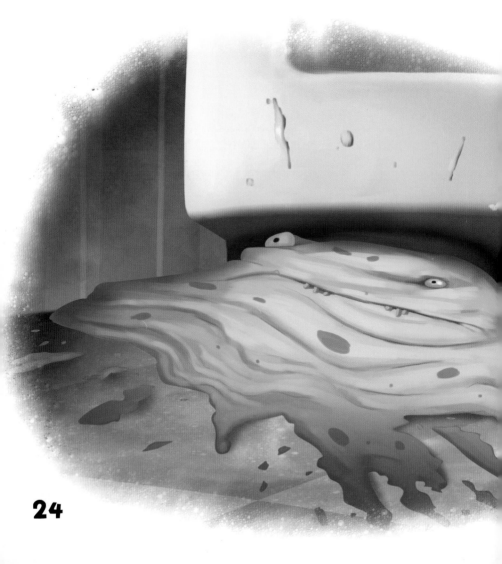

Thing landed safely and quickly hid under the fridge.

But the Blob hit the kitchen floor hard. Splat! There was a bad, bad smell.

"Oh, no! My wonderful smelly cheese!" cried a loud voice. A hand picked up the broken Blob from the floor.

"Cheese?" said Thing to herself, hiding in the dark. "The Blob was made of cheese?"

It smelled horrible. But Thing picked up a small piece of the Blob that had landed under the fridge. She slowly put it in her mouth. Thing's pea-green eyes went pop! Her gray fuzz stood out. She hopped up and down on the spot.

"Wow!" she shouted. "So this is cheese. I love it! I *love* smelly cheese!"

After that, Thing didn't live in the fridge. Instead she stayed under the fridge. She made friends with the local mice who always shared their cheese. Sometimes they had plain cheese, but Thing liked smelly cheese the best.

On long, dark nights she would tell her friends scary stories. The favorite story was all about Thing herself, the time when she was *The Very Brave Thing in the Fridge.*

cheese with bite
cheese with a sharp, strong flavor

cover
shelter

frosty
very cold and covered with a thin layer of ice

icicle
a long, pointed stick of ice

power
electricity

smelly cheese

cheese with strong smell and flavor, often because the cheese maker adds mold

spuds

potatoes

thick voice

a rough, hoarse voice

thrash

beat, whip

vegetable crisper

vegetable container in a fridge

Looking at a Narrative

Introduction

(Who? What? Where?)

Who? **What?** **Where?**

Thing

The food in a freezer melts, and Thing is born in the slimy mess.

A freezer in a kitchen

Problem

(What happens? What goes wrong? How does the character feel?)

Thing goes down into the fridge and discovers different foods. She meets the Blob, a piece of smelly cheese. The Blob is mean and chases Thing around the fridge.

Resolution
(How the problem is solved)

Thing and the Blob fall out of the fridge. The Blob splats on the floor. Thing tastes a piece of the Blob and discovers that she likes smelly cheese. Thing decides to live under the fridge and eat cheese with the mice.

Transition words to look out for

Now	*After that*	*Instead*
At last	*Soon enough*	*Suddenly*

Adjectives to look out for

angry	*big*	*broken*	*buzzy*
flat	*fresh*	*frozen*	*great*
huge	*pea-green*	*soft*	*sour*
whole	*white*	*frosty*	*pink*
furious	*dark*	*spiky*	*slippery*

Author Susan Knight

My daughter once learned a funny poem about the food lurking in a family's fridge. The best line was, "Growing at the back is Something Still Unknown to Science!" Cleaning a messy freezer after a power failure made me wonder how interesting that "something" might be. I decided it would be ugly, curious, and brave! So I wrote Thing's story.

Illustrator Luke Jurevicius

Bzzzzz